For JP, TM, Big Brother
and Deborah with love.

Copyright © 1991 Peter O'Donnell.

All rights reserved. Published by Scholastic Inc.
by arrangement with ABC.

SCHOLASTIC HARDCOVER is a registered trademark of Scholastic Inc.

Library of Congress Cataloging-in-Publication Data

O'Donnell, Peter.
The moonlit journey / Peter O'Donnell.
p.   cm.

Summary: Three encounters reassure a little boy
who is scared of the dark.

[1. Fear of the dark—Fiction.] I. Title.
PZ7.02245   Mo   1991
[E]—dc20
ISBN 0-590-44655-X

12 11 10 9 8 7 6 5 4 3 2 1   1 2 3 4 5   6/9

Printed in Hong Kong by Imago Services (H.K.) Ltd.

First Scholastic printing, April 1991

The Moonlit Journey

BY PETER O'DONNELL

SCHOLASTIC INC. · NEW YORK

As night fell, a restless wind howled across the countryside. It shook the trees, making them creak, and rattled the windows in the houses.

Thomas looked out of his bedroom window into the dark. He hugged his teddy bear close, afraid of what might be out there in the night.

He listened to the howling and the creaking and the rattling.

He imagined he could hear the howling of wolves. Was that a branch blowing against the window, or a wolf scratching on the glass?

A gust of wind blew the window open. Thomas jumped in fright.

Out in the moonlight stood a little red fox, just like the one in the painting near his bed.

"Are there any wolves out there?" Thomas shouted.

"I don't think so," answered the fox, "but I will take you to ask the stag, the wisest animal in our forest. Come, follow me."

Thomas was afraid but he wanted to know if there were wolves in the forest. He wished that his teddy bear was a giant bear.

He looked down at his bear, and at that very moment the little teddy bear began to grow and grow, until he was nearly as large as Thomas's bedroom. The big bear looked down on Thomas and said in a kindly voice, "Climb upon my back, Thomas, and together we will follow the fox."

Thomas held on tightly to the bear's long fur and, with big, soft steps, the mighty bear climbed through the window into the night.

Above them, the wind pushed clouds northwards
across the moon. "Go north, clouds, go north," it
seemed to call. By its light, Thomas and the bear
followed the fox.

The fox led the way under a canopy of branches, while bats played and badgers dug. Thomas held on to the bear's fur.

Finally, they came upon a clearing. An old stag stepped out from the shadows. "Goodness me! What is a little boy like you doing in the forest so late at night?"

"I have never been out in the night before," explained Thomas. "I thought I heard wolves. Are there any wolves in the forest?"

"At nighttime the world becomes mysterious," replied the stag. "If you hear noises and imagine them to be wolves, then wolves you will see. But once you have seen the world at night for yourself, it will never be so frightening again. My friend the fox will take you to the top of the hill to see the world. Your bear can wait here until you return."

The fox led Thomas into the moonlight, where
he saw his shadow move with him on the ground.
They climbed a small hill, where three white
horses galloped but only two moved.

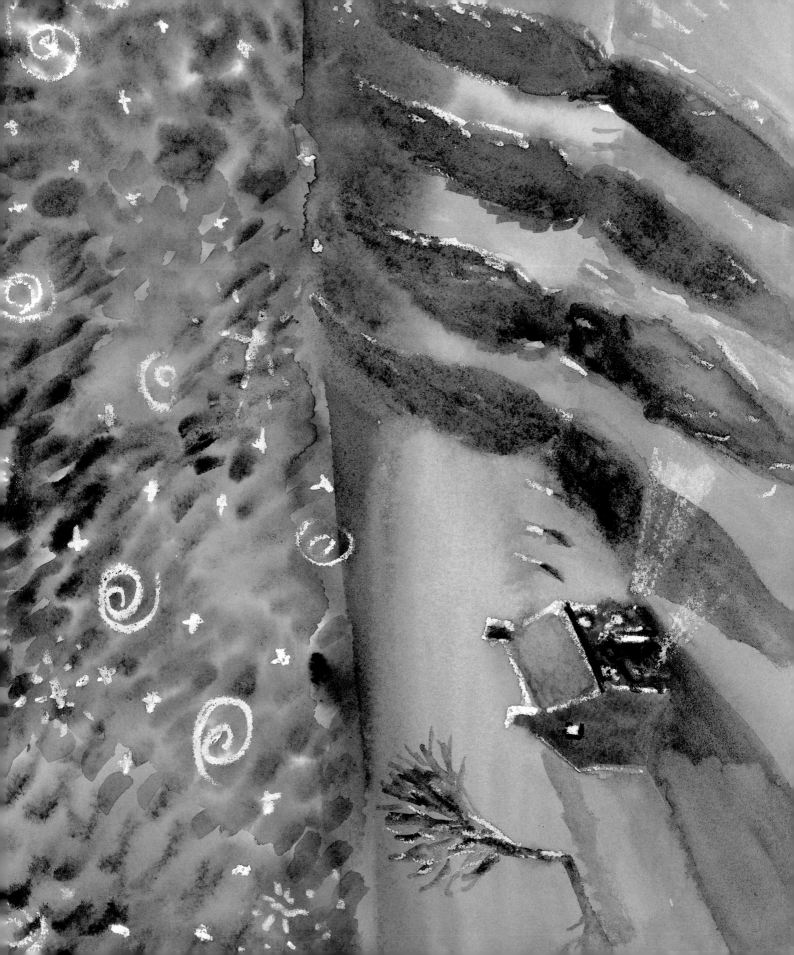

When they reached the top of the hill, all the clouds had been pushed away. A starry sky twinkled. Thomas could see for miles in the moonlight. He could see his own house. But he couldn't see any wolves. "The stag was right," he said to the fox. "Are you sure you've seen enough?" asked the fox.

But Thomas was in such a hurry to tell his bear that he started back.

Soon, he was lost and alone. The forest seemed darker. Thomas was sure the howling wind was wolves. And every shadow looked like a wolf. Maybe there is just one, he thought, or maybe it's a whole pack! There might even be giant wolves!

Thomas began to run and, as he ran, he heard the wolves following him, their paws padding on the ground close behind him.

Suddenly, Thomas bumped into a furry leg and looked up to see his bear.

"What is the matter, Thomas?"

"There are wolves out there, after all. Listen to them howling!"

The bear listened. "All I can hear is the wind in the trees. Perhaps your imagination was running away with you. Let's send the wolves away right now, with mighty sweeps from our paws." He gave a swoosh and all the wolves in Thomas's thoughts tumbled and jumbled and disappeared.

The bear knelt down for Thomas, and the two friends started home, pretending to send wolves flying through the air with mighty paws. The wind had stopped its howling, and the moon shone brightly across the hill, the forest, and the fields.

When they reached the house the bear climbed
quietly into the bedroom.
Together, they curled up beneath the open window
and watched the stars until they fell asleep.